GRASSHOPPER
TO THE RESCUE

A GEORGIAN STORY
Translation from the Russian
by Bonnie Carey
Illustrations by Lady McCrady

William Morrow and Company
New York 1979

Library of Congress Cataloging in Publication Data

Main entry under title:
Grasshopper to the rescue.

    Summary: A cumulative tale describing a grasshopper's attempts to rescue his friend from the river.
    [1. Folklore — Georgia (Transcaucasia)] I. Carey, Bonnie. II. McCrady, Lady.
PZ8.1.G74   [398.2]   [E]   78-11824
ISBN 0-688-22172-6
ISBN 0-688-32172-0 (lib. bdg.)

Printed in the United States of America.
First Edition
1   2   3   4   5   6   7   8   9   10

A grasshopper once made friends with an ant.
They became as close as brothers and set out
together on a journey. Along the way they came
to a river, and the grasshopper said to the ant, "I
will jump across. What about you, brother ant?"

"I'll jump across too!" said the ant.

The grasshopper went *boing*! and jumped across to the other side. But the ant went *phht*! and fell into the water. The river began carrying the poor ant away. "Brother grasshopper," begged the ant, "please help get me out of the water!"

The grasshopper jumped *boing-boing* up to a pig and asked, "Pig, give me some bristles! I will weave a rope out of your bristles, toss the rope into the water, and pull out my friend the ant!"

The pig said, "Feed me some acorns. Then you can take as many of my bristles as you like."

The grasshopper jumped *boing-boing* up to an oak tree and begged, "Oak tree, give me some acorns! I will take the acorns to the pig. The pig will give me some bristles. Then I will weave a rope, toss it into the water, and pull out my friend the ant!"

The oak tree answered, "A raven is sitting on me, cawing and cawing so that I have no peace. Tell him to leave me alone, and I will give you some acorns."

The grasshopper jumped *boing-boing* up to the raven and said, "Raven, leave the oak tree alone! Then the oak will give me acorns, which I will take to the pig. The pig will give me some bristles, and I will weave a rope. I'll toss the rope into the water and pull out my friend the ant!"

The raven said, "Bring me a fresh egg. Then I'll get off the oak tree."

The grasshopper jumped *boing-boing* up to a hen and asked, "Hen, give me an egg! I'll take the egg to the raven so that he'll leave the oak tree alone. The oak tree will give me some acorns, and I'll take the acorns to the pig. Then the pig will give me some bristles so that I can weave a rope. I'll toss the rope into the water and pull out my friend the ant."

The hen said, "Feed me some grain. Then I'll give you an egg."

The grasshopper jumped *boing-boing* up to the barn. "Barn, give me some grain. I'll take the grain to the hen, who will give me an egg. I'll take the egg to the raven, and the raven will leave the oak tree alone. Then the oak tree will give me some acorns, which I'll take to the pig. The pig will give me some bristles, and I'll weave a rope with them. I'll toss the rope into the water and pull out my friend the ant."

The barn spoke in a squeaky voice, "I am bothered by a mouse. She gnaws at me on all sides. Tell her not to gnaw at me, and I'll give you the grain."

The grasshopper jumped *boing-boing* up to the mouse. "Mouse, leave the barn alone! Then the barn will give me some grain, which I will take to the hen. The hen will give me an egg, which I will take to the raven. The raven will leave the oak tree alone so that the oak will give me some acorns. I'll take the acorns to the pig, and the pig will give me some bristles. I'll weave a rope with the bristles, toss it into the water, and pull out my friend the ant."

The mouse said, "Tell the cat not to chase me. Then I won't gnaw the barn anymore. As it is, I only gnaw at it out of nervousness, because I'm afraid of the cat."

The grasshopper jumped *boing-boing* up to the cat. "Cat, don't run after the mouse! Then the mouse won't gnaw the barn, and the barn will give me some grain. I'll take the grain to the hen, who will give me an egg. I'll take the egg to the raven, and he'll leave the oak tree alone. The oak will give me acorns, which I'll take to the pig, and the pig will give me some bristles. I'll weave a rope with the bristles, toss it into the water, and pull out my friend the ant."

The cat replied, "Bring me some milk, and I will stop chasing the mouse."

The grasshopper jumped *boing-boing* up to the cow. "Cow, give me some milk! Then I'll take the milk to the cat, and she will stop chasing the mouse. The mouse will stop gnawing on the barn, and the barn will give me some grain, which I will take to the hen. The hen will give me an egg. I'll take the egg to the raven, who will then leave the oak tree alone. The oak will give me some acorns, which I'll take to the pig. The pig will give me some bristles from which I'll weave a rope. I'll toss the rope into the water and pull out my friend the ant."

The cow said, "Bring me some grass. Then I'll give you some milk."

The grasshopper jumped *boing-boing-*BOING! He rushed to a field, picked some grass, and brought it to the cow. The cow gave him some milk.

The grasshopper took the milk and gave it to the cat. The cat stopped chasing the mouse.

The mouse stopped her gnawing and left the barn alone.

The barn gave the grasshopper some grain.

He took the grain to the hen, and the hen gave
him an egg.

He took the egg to the raven, and the raven left
the oak tree.

The oak tree gave the grasshopper some acorns,
which he took to the pig.

Then the pig gave the grasshopper some bristles.

The grasshopper wove a long rope out of the bristles, fastened a blade of grass to it, and tossed it into the water."

"Hold tight, brother ant!"

The ant grabbed hold of the blade of grass. The grasshopper pulled on the rope and dragged the ant onto the shore. After they rested awhile, they continued on their journey.